Slam Dunk Series

Sixth Man Switch

Tess Eileen Kindig
Illustrated by Joe VanSeveren

For Dandi Mackall,
who knows all the many reasons why

Slam Dunk Series

Sixth Man Switch

Spider McGhee and the Hoopla

Zip, Zero, Zilch

Muggsy Makes an Assist

Gimme an "A"!

March Mania

Double Whammy!

Camp Bee-a-Champ

Published by Concordia Publishing House
3558 S. Jefferson Avenue, St. Louis, MO 63118-3968
Manufactured in the United States of America

Library of Congress Cataloging-in-Publication Data
Kindig, Tess Eileen.
Sixth man switch/ Tess Eileen Kindig.
p. cm. -- (Slam dunk series)
Summary: Mickey, the shortest boy in the forth grade, is excited about the new basketball team being formed for kids his age, but he figures that it will take a miracle from Jesus for him to land a spot on the team.
ISBN 0-570-07163-
[1.Basketball--Fiction. 2.Christian life--Fiction.] I.Title.

PZ7 .K5663 Si 2000
[Fic]--dc21 99-046934

2 3 4 5 6 7 8 9 10 11 09 08 07 06 05 04 03 02 01 00

Contents

One Extra-Large Miracle to Go

ATTENTION BOYS!
Basketball Teams Now Forming
Grades 4–6
Have Fun!
Make Friends!
Get Fit!

"Hey, look!" my best friend Zack Zeno shouted, pointing to the sign on the red brick wall of the city pool house. "Just what we've been waiting for!"

I shoved a weird black rock I'd found on the ground into the side pocket of my jeans and went over to check it out.

"Tryouts are Saturday morning," I read. "We're in, buddy!" I slapped him a high five and we pretended to do a jump shot.

Zack and I are total basketball freaks. Someday we're going to be high school hotshots. Then college all-stars. Then NBA pros. We've got it all planned. But until now we figured we'd have to wait until sixth grade to play on a real team.

"Hey!" somebody hollered from the parking lot next to the pool house.

It brought our feet down hard on the sidewalk. Every time I hear that voice I feel like I just got punched in the stomach. I could be at a real live Bull's game and the sound of that know-it-all tone would spoil the whole thing. Michael Jordan could sink a winning three-pointer and I'd be feeling sicker than the winner of a pie-eating contest.

"Hey, Sam!" I hollered back. I always pretend like Sam Sherman doesn't get to me. But it's getting harder and harder to do. Not only does he make my life miserable, but he also gets everything he wants. He even gets everything *I* want, which right now includes a dog and being tall enough to play center.

I know the last one will never happen, but I might actually get a dog someday. At least that's what my mom says. Trouble is, she's been saying it for two years already and "someday" is no closer than it ever was.

"You guys trying out for the team?" Sam asked. He came toward us, dribbling what looked like a brand new basketball. His huge black Lab, Zorro, pranced along beside him sporting a bright red collar.

"We might," Zack said.

"Yeah, we might," I agreed.

Sam dribbled the ball under his leg and lost control of it. It rolled off the sidewalk into the grass.

Zack and I grinned as he ran after it.

Sam picked up the ball and walked the rest of the way to the pool house. "You'd better get in some serious practice then," he warned. "Most of the guys who have a chance to make the team were at basketball camp this summer."

My heart sank. Well, not really. That's just a thing people say when they're upset. But if hearts *could* sink, mine would have ended up somewhere around my ankles. Sam was right. At the end of last year, a player from the local pro team came to our school and passed out flyers about the camp. Everyone who was serious about basketball signed up. Except for Zack and me. Basketball camp cost more than $100. Even without asking, we knew our parents couldn't afford it.

"We don't need basketball camp," I said now, heading toward my bike. "We're naturals."

"Naturals!" Sam scoffed. He laughed so hard he doubled up over the ball. "When's the last time you looked in the mirror, McGhee?" he asked me. "You're a little shrimp."

I picked up my bike from the ground where I'd crashed it and jumped on. Already I could feel my ears burning. It was like Sam Sherman held a remote control. All he had to do was press a button, and I turned as red as a sunburn. I'm the shortest boy in the fourth grade. Most of the *girls* are even taller than I am.

"Size doesn't matter," Zack said loyally, jumping on his bike too. "Mickey's got speed."

I didn't say anything. Sam was showing off his crossover dribble. It was so fast and clean, you could set it to music. He'd sure learned a lot at that basketball camp.

Zorro barked and ran in little circles as the ball bounced across the concrete. Usually I like to watch Zorro, but not today. I rode off toward home with Zack behind me. We didn't talk until we crossed the street and were safely in our own neighborhood. Then he rode up alongside me.

"Don't let him get to you," he said. "We're in. We're in!"

"I know," I agreed. But I wasn't so sure anymore.

At my house, I turned onto the bumpy gravel driveway and Zack followed. Our old ten-speeds rattled like two jars of marbles. We squeezed our handbrakes and came to a stop, sending the gravel flying.

"Want to do a little one-on-one before supper?" Zack asked.

"OK." I dropped my bike and got my basketball from the garage. I'd told my mom I'd clean my room after school, but maybe if I didn't go into the house, she'd forget for awhile.

I bounced the ball a few times on the pad by the side door of the house. The thud, thud, thud sound it made slapping against the fresh concrete made my muscles unclench. My dad and I had just poured that pad two weeks ago. We built the frame and everything. When the cement was ready, Dad mounted a metal pole in the ground to hold the basket. Later Zack and I painted it black. Nobody could even tell it used to be a city light-pole we got for free.

I tossed the ball to Zack and he pivoted wildly in all directions, trying to freak me out.

"Dee-fense! Dee-fense!" I shouted, trying to block with my arms.

Zack laughed and shot over my head. The ball hit the rim and bounced off. We both scrambled for it.

"Hi, Mickey!"

I froze, both hands on the ball. There's only one other voice besides Sam Sherman's that can stop me cold, and this was it. I let go of the ball and straightened up.

"Hi, Trish," I said.

Trish Riley lives down the street and sits in front of me in Mrs. Clay's class. It's totally embarrassing to admit this, but she has a monster crush on me. I hate it. Neither Zack nor I want to get involved with girls. At least not until we're 27. Maybe even 30!

She pulled the brim of the baseball cap she always wears down over her forehead and smiled. "You're really good, Mickey. I bet you make the team."

Zack pretended like he was practicing his speed dribble. But I could see his shoulders shaking up and down from laughing. Good? What did Trish Riley know about good? I'd just let Zack complete a throw that should have gone in easy.

"Thanks." I turned back to Zack, but Trish made no move to leave.

"I guess you heard about Sam Sherman," she said.

"What about him?" I could feel my muscles tensing up again.

Now that she had my attention, Trish walked up the driveway. "Last Saturday he landed a pair of baskets in front of 2000 people at an exhibition game."

"Huh?" Suddenly I was all ears.

She nodded. "It's true. He went up to State to see his brother play. His brother's a big star at the university, you know."

Zack stopped dribbling and came over. "Sam Sherman didn't play at any State game," he said.

"No way. No way!" But you could tell he wasn't sure.

Now that she had Zack's attention too, Trish continued her story. "Yes, he did," she said, yanking on her baseball cap again. That's something she does whenever she talks to me. "At halftime they toss T-shirts into the crowd. If you catch one, you get to go down on the floor and shoot. Sam grabbed one, raced down there and shot two baskets right in a row. No misses."

Zack and I exchanged glances. I knew he was thinking the same thing I was. *How thrilling it would be to hear the crowd roaring its approval, especially for a fourth grader.*

"Oh yeah? So what?" I said, reaching down for the ball Zack had left on the ground.

Trish saw she was losing us. "He won a real prize too," she added. "Got a whole wad of coupons for free food. Burgers, shakes, fries, all kind of free stuff."

We let that sink in. Rarely did we get to eat fast food. I couldn't even remember when I'd last wrapped my mouth around a bacon cheeseburger. But that wasn't the important part. The big thing was Sam Sherman out on the court shooting baskets at a college game.

Zack and I looked at each other again. We didn't even have to say it.

We were dead.

Behind me a window squeaked open on the side of the house. "Mickey McGhee! You get in here and clean your room this minute!" my mom shouted.

Red crawled up my neck and stained my face like cherry Kool-Aid. "I gotta go," I mumbled.

I picked up my bike, tossed the basketball in the dented wire basket and wheeled the bike up the driveway to the garage. "See ya, Zack!" I called. I didn't say good-bye to Trish. It's not that I was trying to be rude or anything. I just didn't want her getting any more ideas than she already had.

Our garage is only big enough for one car. So I always have to make sure to get my bike tight against the wall so my dad doesn't drive his pick-up into it. I did that, then walked back toward the house.

In my head I could hear the college band playing "Hang On Sloopy" during halftime. I could smell the nachos and taste the icy blast of freshly poured pop. But mostly, I could feel the excitement crackling like wrapping paper around an Easter basket, as Sam Sherman strutted his stuff on the wide, polished floor.

It made me groan right out loud. We were only kidding ourselves. For Zack Zeno and Mickey McGhee to land a spot on the basketball team it was going to take a miracle!

On the scale of, say, the loaves and the fishes. Or the wedding feast of Cana.

In other words, a real doozy!

Only Jesus could pull off something that big!

2

Backed into a Corner

Thud! Scriiiiitch!

I dived under my pillow and jammed it down tight over my ears. Every morning at exactly 7:00, my mother pushes open the door to my room. The sound is worse than the shrill of the buzzer at the end of a losing game. A 100-year-old door in a 100-year-old house was never meant to be dragged across wall-to-wall carpeting.

"Mickey! Time to get up!" she called.

"I'm up already," I mumbled into the mattress. I say that nearly every day. Most of the time I even believe it. What happens is, I sort of half doze off and see myself getting dressed, brushing my teeth, and walking down the stairs. And I think I'm really doing it. Then I wake up, and there I am, still sandwiched between the sheets like a slice of salami.

This morning I didn't feel like catching any more "Z's" though. Ever since I had heard about Sam Sherman shooting those baskets at State, it was like I had Mexican jumping beans under my skin. When I wasn't shooting real baskets, I was shooting air balls practically every minute of the day.

"Good morning, God," I said out loud as my feet hit the floor. That's something else I do every day. Even when I'm late, which is almost always, I still say hi to God first thing.

I grabbed my sneakers by their laces and started to yank them out from under the bed. Wham!—a terrible thought froze me as still as a statue. I had forgotten something. Something BIG. And I didn't have a clue what it was.

"Hi, Mickey," my little sister Meggie said from the doorway. She'd tried to fix the torn ruffle of her Beauty and the Beast nightgown with tape, but it still drooped around her ankles. "Mama says don't forget it's your day to help at the co-op after school." She stared at me. "What's the matter? You look funny."

I ignored the question. The co-op is where we buy most of our food. Once a month, the basement of the church turns into a grocery store. A big truck drops off barrels of food that get divided up into plastic bags. Then the people who belong to the co-op come to pick up what they had ordered.

Mom says co-op food is better for you because it doesn't have chemicals. But I think the real reason we shop there is because it's cheaper, especially if you volunteer to help. Usually she does it, but when she can't, I'm the one who gets stuck working. Last time I spent two whole hours just counting apples. But as bad as working at the co-op was, I knew it wasn't the thing I had forgotten.

"May I ride my bike to school?" I asked when I got down to the kitchen. Usually the answer is "no" because of this one busy street I have to cross. But I always try.

"Yes, but only because of the co-op," Mom answered, surprising me. She poured a bowl of cereal from a plastic co-op bag for me, and started reciting her famous "Wooster Street Rule." "And you have to promise me you'll get off at Wooster and walk your bike across at the light. It's too dangerous for you to ride across four lanes of traffic. OK?"

"Yeah, sure. No problem," I said, pouring milk on the pile of flakes in my bowl.

Walking my bike is babyish, but if it meant not having to take the bus, I'd do it. Sam Sherman's buddies are always on the bus bragging about stuff Zack and I don't have or can't do. I wished I could call Zack and have him ride his bike too, but I couldn't. His dad works nights and is just getting to sleep when Zack leaves for school. He hates it when the phone rings in the morning.

Outside, I pedaled hard down Arvin Avenue and hung a left onto Greenwood. The cold air whizzing past my ears cleared the morning fuzz out of my head. If only I could remember what I'd forgotten!

Maybe it had something to do with basketball. Before tryouts, I would have to work on making better passes. My problem is that I always hog the ball until I'm in trouble. Then I wind up shoving it at whomever is close by. Usually it turns out to be the one player most likely to drop it. When you want to be a star, like I do, passing is a skill that doesn't come naturally. But my dad says …

I jammed on the brakes so hard I nearly fell off my bike. Passing! School! Language arts! The thing I had forgotten came hurtling back at me faster than a rebound. Today was the day we had to read our essays about goals in front of the class!

I rested my head on the handlebars of my ten-speed and groaned out loud. I had plenty of goals. What I *didn't* have was an essay. All I needed was for Mrs. Clay to call my mom and tell her I was messing up in school and the closest I'd ever get to the basketball team would be the bleachers.

"Hey, Mickey! Wait up!"

I groaned louder. The last person I wanted to talk to at a time like this was Trish Riley.

She pulled alongside of me on her pink and

purple bike and screeched to a stop. "What's the matter? You don't look so great," she said, tugging on the brim of her baseball cap. It was a dumb girlie cap today—hot pink like her bike.

"Did you write your essay?" I asked, ignoring both the insult and the hat.

She nodded. "Yep. I wrote about how I'm going to be a teacher like my mom. What did you write about, Mickey?"

I considered letting her think I had written about basketball, but I didn't. She'd find out the truth soon enough. "That's the trouble," I said. "I sort of forgot it was due today."

"Uh-oh." She thought about that. Then she looked at her pink watch and let out a squeal. It was loud enough to blast a hole through my eardrum. "Mickey! You can still do it! We've got 15 whole minutes."

Before I could correct the *we*, she hopped off her bike. She hit the kickstand and started rooting around in her purple backpack. "Look, I've got notebook paper," she said, handing me a short stack.

I stared at it, then looked up and down the street. It was early. There weren't too many kids walking by yet. Maybe if I hurried …

"But I don't have anything to write on. No book or anything. I need something hard," I said.

Trish grinned. "You can write on my back," she said. She sounded like she'd just won the Publisher's Clearinghouse Sweepstakes. "I'll sit really, really still and not say a word while you write." She plopped down on the grass to show me how quiet she could be.

I looked around again. A couple of morning kindergarten kids were coming around the corner with their moms, but that was all. With my whole future hanging on this essay, I couldn't afford to worry about kindergarten babies, or Trish Riley's bony back.

"OK." I dropped my bike on the grass and grabbed a sharp yellow No. 2 pencil out of my own backpack. Then I knelt down behind her, and put the paper up against her pink jacket.

Right away I started writing. It was so easy, it didn't even seem like homework. I wrote about how I was going to be on the team. About high school and college and the NBA. And even about how I was going to have a big dog that would chase basketballs and do tricks. By the time I was done, I had filled both sides of the paper.

"Got it!" I yelled, shoving it into my backpack.

Before Trish could get to her feet, I jumped on my bike and sped off. "Thanks!" I hollered over my shoulder. The next time I saw her, the tardy bell was ringing and she was flying in the door with her hat on sideways.

"I hope you all worked hard on your essays," our teacher, Mrs. Clay, said during language arts. "I think it will be fun to hear everyone's dreams."

Kristy Shaw went first. She's the most popular girl in the whole fourth grade, not just in our class. If I were interested in girls—which I'm definitely not—I would think Kristy was sort of cute. She read an essay about being a supermodel. It was sort of boring, but so were everybody else's essays. By the time it was my turn I wasn't even nervous. Compared to being a supermodel, an astronaut, a lawyer, a magician, or a horse whisperer, being a basketball player sounded pretty cool.

"I have many goals," I read in a loud, clear voice. "But the most important one is my goal to be a professional basketball player."

In the back row, Sam Sherman let out a loud snort. Mrs. Clay shot him a frown and shook her head no. (He was lucky it was early. If he'd done that in the afternoon when she was tired, she'd have yelled at him for sure!)

"It doesn't matter which team I end up on," I read. I shifted from one foot to the other and kept my eyes on the page. "But I wouldn't mind if it were the Chicago Bulls. The Bulls are awesome. Before I can think about such a far away goal, though, I need to reach my first goal. I need to make the rec department basketball team."

Sam snorted even louder. Mrs. Clay moved to the back of the room. I cleared my throat and slicked down the dumb piece of hair on the top of my head. It always sticks up like a soldier standing at attention.

"I play a really mean defense," I continued. "I practice every minute I get. It isn't enough for me to just make the team though. I want to be a star."

Sam erupted like a geyser. Before Mrs. Clay could do anything, the whole room sounded like a TV laugh track.

"That's enough!" Mrs. Clay snapped.

The laughing stopped, but I knew everybody was still imagining shrimpy Mickey McGhee running around the court with giants like Magic Johnson and Shaquille O'Neal. Only Trish and Zack weren't laughing. Trish turned around and glared at Sam.

"Sam, if you can't be polite, I think you had better sit out in the hall for the rest of the period," Mrs. Clay said in her normal voice.

Usually I would have been glad to see Sam Sherman get booted out of class, but not today. Today I wished I could be the one slinking out to the hall.

Sam got up and slouched out the door. His face

was as pink as a petunia. Mine was redder than a burning bush. I finished reading the rest of my essay about the dog I would get when I was famous. When I walked back to my seat Zack gave me the "thumbs up" sign. I wished the boards of the floor would part like the Red Sea and swallow me up.

Maybe it *was* stupid to think I could play in the NBA. Maybe it was even *more* stupid to think I could make the rec department team. Maybe I should just quit before things got any worse.

At lunch I got my tray and followed Zack to our table in the corner. We had to pass Sam, but I didn't look at him. He and his friends were talking about jump shots and layups. When they saw me, they started laughing like hyenas. Right away I could feel my ears copying the color of the sauce on my spaghetti. If there's a person in the whole U.S.A. who blushes more than I do, I'd sure like to meet him.

"Hey, McGhee," Sam said as I went by. "I didn't know you had a girlfriend."

"Huh?" I stared at him.

"I saw you writing on Trish Riley's back this morning," he said, smirking. "What was it—your famous NBA story?"

"Ignore him," Zack called in front of me.

I tried, but the whole table hooted. Maybe it

was a good thing I had to go to the co-op tonight, I decided, as I flopped into a chair at the lunch table. I'd had it up to my tomato red ears with basketball for one day!

Walking on Walnuts

I leaned my bike against the side of the church and looked around the parking lot. Two tattooed men with arms the size of logs were locking up the back of the semi that had delivered the food for the co-op. Already I could picture what it looked like in the church basement with all that stuff waiting to get bagged. Now that I was actually at the co-op, basketball was starting to look good to me again.

"Mickey! Sweetie! Your mom said to expect you," Mrs. Samples, the woman in charge, gushed as I walked in. She's a nice lady, but she's always calling me embarrassing stuff like "Sweetie" or "Honey," and sometimes even "Babe."

"Hi, Mrs. Samples," I said politely. My eyes popped at the sight of a metal table covered with what looked like three million acorn squash. "Uh—is it OK if my friend Zack Zeno helps too? He had to go home and tell his dad first, but he's coming over later."

"That's fine, hon. You boys can bag macaroni."

She got up and led me across the room to a huge wooden barrel filled to the brim with pasta elbows. Then she handed me a metal scoop. "Eight big scoops to a bag," she said, pointing to the pile of clear plastic bags on the table next to the barrel.

I already knew the drill. Once, back in the summer, I'd scooped goldfish crackers. The good thing about scooping is that while your arm is busy filling bags your mind can be playing a close game against the Utah Jazz.

But today I thought about Sam Sherman and how he had made the whole class laugh at me. When you got right down to it, it wasn't really all that different from when the crowds had laughed at Jesus on the cross. Guess He'd showed them in the end. Maybe I needed to show Sam Sherman something too. The thought filled me with so much energy I even started whistling. If you happen to like "Yankee Doodle," I'm a pretty good whistler.

"Hi, Mickey."

I stopped in mid-note. That voice had already gotten me in enough trouble for one day. What was it doing at the co-op, of all places?

"Hi, Trish," I said, scooping up an extra-big bunch of macaroni. "I didn't expect to see you here." I hoped that didn't sound rude, but after this morning, she was starting to wear on my nerves!

"I heard you tell Zack you had to go to the church to help with the co-op, so I came over to tell you something," she said. If she noticed I wasn't exactly thrilled to see her, she didn't let on. She was so excited she was practically jumping out of her freckled skin. "Guess what?"

I was afraid to ask, so I didn't.

"I made the cheerleading squad!" She flashed me a grin so wide I could see the clips that held the rubber bands on her front teeth. "For your basketball games," she explained when I didn't say anything. "Isn't that great?"

Oh, yeah, great. That's the word I'd use, all right. But I worked up a smile and said I was happy for her. It wasn't even a lie. I *was* happy for her. It was ME I wasn't so happy for.

"Want to see me cheer?" she asked.

"Uh, that's OK. Surprise me," I mumbled. Already I could feel the tops of my ears getting hot. I looked around the room. Everybody was busy working. Two more volunteers had just come in, so Mrs. Samples was showing them how to gather orders. I wondered what was taking Zack so long.

Looking back on it, I guess surprise was the wrong word to have used. Because a surprise is exactly what Trish Riley gave me. Before I could stop her, she lunged forward on one knee and punched out her fist.

"Gimme an M!" she shouted.

The macaroni scoop fell out of my hand and clattered to the cement floor.

Trish jumped back and slapped her arm down straight at her side. "Gimme an I! Gimme a C!" she hollered, lunging forward again. This time she punched with her left arm, sending me backing up against the wall flatter than a coat of paint.

I squeezed my eyes into slits and prayed this wasn't happening.

It was happening.

Trish gave the air three fast punches in a row and yelled, "Gimme a K-E-Y! GO-OOOOOOO, MICKEY!" Then she did a forward flip.

Her feet shot toward my head like two white missiles. I let out a yelp, ducked, and jumped—straight into a rickety set of metal shelves filled with food. For a second, they swayed like a tree in the wind. I grabbed them with both hands and pushed them back against the wall. But not before a huge white cardboard box pitched forward off the top.

The next thing I knew something hard—*lots* of something hard—were pouring over my head and pelting my shoulders. I screamed and tried to block the shower with my arms, but it kept right on coming.

"Ow! Ow! Owwwwwwwww!"

"Mickey! Ohhhhhhhhh, Mickey!"

That was Trish, but I only sort of heard it. By the time the shower of hard things stopped, I was smack in the middle of a crowd of ladies.

Ladies who did not look happy.

I blinked and looked down at the hard things skittering across the cement like little brown mice. It had rained walnuts. The kind still in their dimpled shells.

"Young man, you will need to pick up every single one of those nuts," an old lady with blue frizzy hair and a bright purple sweater said. You could tell by her tone that she used to be a teacher.

"Yes, ma'am," I replied, staring miserably at the floor. There were enough walnuts there to stuff every Christmas stocking in the city. I grabbed the empty box, sank to my knees, and started grabbing whole fistfuls of nuts. I was glad nobody could see my face.

"I'll help you, Mickey," Trish offered. She crouched down beside me and started gathering walnuts.

A couple of them had landed near the table leg to my right. I reached over to get them. Trish reached for them at the exact same second. Crash! Our heads banged together like two bowling pins.

"Owwwwwwww!" I howled. It hurt so bad, I completely forgot that I was trying not to attract any more attention.

Trish burst into tears.

The lady with the frizzy blue hair stopped bagging lemons and came back over. She said to Trish in her teacher voice, "Young lady, I think it would be wise for you to go home now."

Trish scrubbed at her eyes with her fists and sniffed loudly. I sort of felt sorry for her. Trish Riley doesn't mean to be a pain. It's just the way she is.

"She was only trying to help. Honest," I said to the lady.

Trish got up and ran toward the stairs. I could hear her sneakers pounding on the steps all the way up. I sank back against my feet on the floor and wondered why this sort of stuff always happens to me. I try to mind my own business and do what I'm supposed to do, and stuff like this just happens. It's a mystery.

After I cleaned up the walnuts and went back to bagging macaroni, I started seriously wondering where Zack was. The clock on the wall by the kitchen said 4:00 already. He should have been here at least 15 minutes ago. I sure hoped his dad hadn't made him stay home and do homework or something.

"Mickey, sweetie," Mrs. Samples called from across the room. "Do you think you could reach behind you and bring me that big sack of flour?"

I stopped scooping and looked at the rickety metal shelves. A lot of white powdery stuff filled a clear plastic bag. If it had been down on the floor, it would have come up to my knees at least. That *had* to be the flour. I reached up and hefted it down.

"Is it too heavy, darlin'?" she called.

"I've got it!" I hollered back. It must have weighed at least 20 pounds, but I had a strong grip on it. As I lugged the bag across the room, I thought maybe Zack had forgotten he was supposed to come over here. Maybe he'd started watching cartoons, or maybe he'd gone over to the rec center to shoot a few hoops. That last thought bugged me. A good friend wouldn't even think about shooting hoops with the enemy at a time like …

It happened fast. Faster than a hard drive to the basket. My shoe hit something hard and round and down I went—clutching the sack of flour to my chest like a basketball.

"Ahhh, ahhh, ahhh-choo!" A monster sneeze ripped through my lungs and out my nose like an explosion. I'm here to tell you—until you've had flour fly up your nose you don't know what a sneeze is! The bag had split right up the middle. Most of the flour was still inside, but a fine cloud drifted up to my face. Without even looking, I knew what I looked like. A loaf of bakery bread that had just been dusted.

The blue-haired lady in the purple sweater came towards me with her hands on her hips. I held my breath and waited for what I knew was coming. She was going to throw me out of the co-op. She was going to tell me that if I couldn't be trusted with simple jobs like scooping macaroni or carrying flour, I was clearly not co-op material.

But before she could say it, two feet pounded down the stairs like something—or someone—was chasing them. Zack burst into sight, taking the last three steps in one leap.

"Help! Somebody! Come quick!" he cried. "There's been an accident!"

4

Faced with Fear (and Flour)

I wiggled out from under the bag of flour and stared at Zack, but he was so freaked I don't think he even saw me.

"Quick! In the parking lot!" he cried, taking off up the steps again with Mrs. Samples right behind him.

For a second, I couldn't move. I thought about picking up the flour sack. But in the end, I left it and ran after them. My heart was pounding in my chest like the bass on a teenager's car radio. Deep in my bones I knew this accident had something to do with me.

On the top step I tripped and landed on all fours. By the time I picked myself up and burst through the door, both Zack and Mrs. Samples were down on their knees bent over something. It was lying on the strip of grass in front of the hedge that divided the church's property from the house next door.

"What is it? What's wrong?" I yelled. But before they could answer, I already knew. An animal was yelping in pain. The sound of it gave me the shakes.

"It's a puppy," Zack called, not looking at me. "He was run over by a car."

I fell to my knees on the grass beside Zack and sucked in my breath. The littlest dog I've ever seen in my life was lying there covered with blood. Without thinking, I reached out to pet his fuzzy brown and tan head.

"Don't touch him, Mickey," Mrs. Samples warned before I made contact. "He might bite. He's really hurt. We need to get help."

I knew better than to touch an injured animal. Two days a week my mom works at the Humane Society, so I've been around animals since I was a little kid. I just wasn't thinking straight. All I could see was how miserable and helpless the poor little guy was. It made me want to pick him up and take off running to the nearest vet. As soon as Mrs. Samples said "help" though, my brain clicked into gear. I stopped shaking and jumped to my feet.

"Today's the day the vet comes to the Humane Society," I told them. "We can take him there. Wait here! I know how to move him."

Now that I had taken charge, it was like my feet were motorized. I zipped inside and ripped a cardboard flap off a grocery box. Then I grabbed my jacket and an empty burlap sack. I tore back out to the parking lot.

Breathing hard, I said to Mrs. Samples, "Here, wrap this sack around your hands, slide the cardboard under him, and ease him onto it. Then cover him with my jacket. Even his face. You can lift him up and he won't bite you." I knew what to do. I'd seen my mom move injured animals at least a half-dozen times.

The puppy wailed as the cardboard slid under his small broken body, but Mrs. Samples was able to get him onto it and lift him off the ground. She headed for her car and Zack and I followed. At the car, she handed me the cardboard with the dog while she reached into the pocket of her jeans for her keys.

"Let us go along," I pleaded as I looked down at the puppy. He was barely moving under my old denim jacket. "Please, Mrs. Samples. You'll need somebody to hold him."

Before she could say "no," Zack climbed into the backseat, and I got in front, carefully setting the cardboard on my lap. The puppy had stopped yelping and was now whimpering softly.

Don't let him die. Don't let him die. Don't let him die ... The words played over and over in my head. It was the biggest prayer I'd ever said in my life!

Gently I lifted back the collar of my jacket and looked at the puppy's face. His big brown eyes rolled to the side and stared straight into mine. My heart did a flip. It was like he was pleading with me to make the pain stop. I think at that second I'd have given up a spot on the basketball team to help him. I took a deep, shaky breath and kept on praying.

"Hurry," I begged when Mrs. Samples stopped at the traffic light in front of the church. "Hurry!" But the light stayed red forever. "CHANGE!" I screamed at it. "Change, you dumb light!"

Mrs. Samples drove as fast as she could without causing a wreck, but it still seemed like three years before we pulled into the parking lot of the Humane Society.

"Run inside and let them know we're here!" I hollered to Zack who was already halfway across the concrete.

Carefully, I eased myself and the injured dog out of the car and headed toward the door. Just as I got there, Dr. Barry, the vet, came up the steps from the basement with Zack at her heels. Without a word, she took the dog from me and disappeared into an examining room.

When the door closed, my heart took a nose-dive. Couldn't Dr. Barry see the dog was too scared to be alone? Couldn't she see that he needed me?

Mrs. Samples put her arm around my shoulders. "Come on, babe," she said, leading me away. "The doctor needs room to work." She led me to a row of chairs and Zack followed. For once "babe" actually sounded kind of good. Of course, I wouldn't have admitted it in front of the guys at school if you'd have pulled out my fingernails and gave me Chinese Water Torture.

"Did you see him get hit?" I asked Zack as I sat on the edge of one of the chairs. "Did the driver know what happened? Was it a hit and run?" I knew I was babbling. But if I didn't talk, I'd start crying and never stop.

Zack nodded. "I didn't exactly see it," he said. "But it was a hit and run all right. I heard the thud when it got hit, and I saw a flashy, red car tear out of the lot like lightning. It couldn't get out of there fast enough!"

"Did you happen to see the license plate?" Mrs. Samples asked.

Zack scrunched up his face trying to remember. "Yeah. No. I mean, sort of. I saw the first two letters. They were M and S and then I think maybe a three. But I don't know after that."

"We need to file a police report," Mrs. Samples said. "You boys wait here. I'm going to call the police department. Whoever did this, needs to own up to it. You said a flashy, red car, right?"

Zack nodded. Right then I didn't care one bit about flashy, red cars. All I cared about was the dog. All my life I have wanted a dog. Every Christmas and every birthday I ask for one, but I never get one. My mom keeps saying "someday." She also says I have basketball on the brain and wouldn't take care of it, just like I don't take care of my room. But I would! I know it! Dogs and rooms are two totally different things.

"Do—do you think he's going to die, Mrs. Samples?" I asked. My voice cracked, but I didn't even care.

"I don't know, honey," she said, giving me a hug. "I don't know." She grabbed some change from her pocket and headed for the pay phone on the wall by the door.

We had to wait a long time for Dr. Barry to come out with any news. Even Zack was quiet for a change. The whole time I kept praying. *Please God, don't let the dog die. Please God. He's so little. He needs me. I need him too. Please God.*

By the time Mrs. Samples came back from calling the police, I felt like I couldn't sit still another minute.

"Mickey, I called your mom and told her not to worry," Mrs. Samples said, sitting down in a chair beside me. "We need to run by the police station on the way home and make out a report. She said that was fine. I also called the church and told them we wouldn't be back."

The co-op seemed like 100 years ago. Even Trish Riley's cheerleading didn't bother me anymore. All I wanted was for the dog to somehow live. I continued praying.

Then, suddenly, I thought of something so amazing it made me catch my breath. Maybe the reason I had never gotten a dog before, was because I was supposed to have this dog!

"You OK, sweetheart?" Mrs. Samples asked when she heard the sharp sound I made when I inhaled.

I nodded. I couldn't put the thought into words. It's not that I was afraid she would laugh or anything. Zack wouldn't laugh either because he knows how much I want a dog of my own. It's just that it was so huge. I wanted to keep it private for awhile—at least until I saw what was going to happen to him.

The sound of Dr. Barry's heels clicking across the floor made me start to shake again. I jumped up and ran toward her.

"Is he OK? Is he going to live?" I asked.

The vet took a deep breath. "I don't know yet, Mickey," she said. She looked me straight in the eye like she thought I was old enough to handle the truth. "We're sure going to try to save him. I came out to tell you to go home now. We need to operate, so we have to go to the animal hospital. They're coming to get him right now. I have managed to stop the bleeding, and I am giving him some medicine through an IV. For the time being, he is at least comfortable. We'll know more in the morning."

I nodded. I didn't want to go home. I didn't even want to go to the police station. The only place I wanted to go was the animal hospital. But I knew I didn't have any choice. I had to do what the doctor ordered.

"OK," I said. "Thanks, Dr. Barry."

Slowly, I followed Mrs. Samples back to the parking lot with Zack beside me. The air was much colder than it had been when we went in. I'd left my jacket with the dog, so right away I started shivering. For a second I thought about going back for it, but I decided not to. It was probably covered with bloodstains. Anyway, I liked the idea of leaving a part of myself behind with him.

"Wow, it's starting to get dark," Zack said as we reached Mrs. Samples beat-up brown car. "We must have been in there a long time."

I hadn't noticed, but Zack was right. It was early evening already. I looked up at the gray sky just as the tall, silver lights around the edge of the parking lot buzzed and flickered on. The sudden burst of light made me blink.

Zack let out a whoop of laughter.

"Wha-at? What's so funny?" I demanded.

"You!" he cried, pointing at me. "Oh, Mick you've gotta see yourself."

Mrs. Samples stopped fumbling with her keys and laughed too. "Darlin', you look like a ghost!" she exclaimed.

As soon as she opened the door, I jumped into the car to get a look at myself in the mirror. My eyes stared back at me huge and round. Against the sickly white of my hair and face, they looked like a pair of Hershey's chocolate kisses. I'd forgotten all about the flour!

5

A Dog's Life

The next morning my mother didn't get a chance to drag the bottom of my door across the carpet. I was out of bed and down the stairs the second I heard her moving around the kitchen.

"Call the animal hospital," I begged, bursting into the room in my pajamas. "I *have* to know if the dog's all right."

Mom glanced at the clock above the table. It's shaped like a grinning black cat with huge, white, people teeth and a long black tail that swishes back and forth with each tick. My dad had given it to her for Christmas. "Mickey, it's 6:30 in the morning," she said, shaking her head. "I can't call over there at this hour."

"But I have to go to school," I pointed out. "How am I going to concentrate if I'm worried about the dog?"

She thought about that while she measured out coffee. "You can call home at lunch, and I'll let you know then." She set down the coffee scoop and reached into the cupboard for the flowered tin where she keeps spare change. "Don't lose this now," she warned, handing me money for the pay phone.

I scowled, but didn't say anything. There was no sense asking her not to treat me like a baby, when I had to convince her to let me keep the dog. If she said yes to the dog, I was almost 100 percent sure my dad would say yes too.

Having a dog would be so great. Especially when I made the team. The newspaper would come to write a story about me and they'd wind up taking a picture of me and my very own dog. Maybe I could teach him how to play basketball. I saw a movie once where a dog could play so well he became a superstar.

The morning dragged by slower than a trip to the dentist. I was supposed to get together with the guys after school and practice before tryouts, but I was too worried to even think about it. I was definitely too worried to think about school. When Mrs. Clay asked me who sewed the first American flag, I almost said, "Dr. Barry."

Finally, the lunch bell shrilled and I tore out the door. I moved so fast, I could have been a cartoon kid with whirling lines around my feet. I had to get to the pay phones before they got jammed up with kids who'd forgotten their homework.

My hand was shaking as I dialed my number.

Mom answered on the second ring.

"The dog made it safely through surgery, Mickey," she said. "But it's still touch and go with an animal that small. We can only hope and pray for the best."

The last part barely made it into my brain. The dog was alive! He'd made it! I grinned and let out a whoop. Mrs. Clay frowned at me, but I was too happy to care. I figured she wouldn't care either once she saw how hard I'd be able to think now that I knew the dog was OK. She was always telling me I could get math if only I thought harder. I was now ready to think until my brain overheated and smoke blew out my ears!

After school Zack and I rode over to Pinecrest Park to meet the other guys from our neighborhood, including Sam Sherman. Sam doesn't really live in our neighborhood. He lives on Adams Street where rich people have started buying the big run-down old houses and fixing them up. Unfortunately, Adams Street is closer to Pinecrest Park than it is to Silver Maple Park, so we get stuck with him. He was already on the outdoor court when we rode up on our bikes.

"Hey, guys!" he called. "Check this!" He dribbled the ball a few times, pivoted, and sank a basket.

Personally, I thought he looked sort of dumb

wearing his brother's basketball shirt with the big number 36 on it. If I'd wanted to, I could have really zapped him. The shirt was long enough to be a dress. Zack and I exchanged grins. I knew he was thinking the same thing.

A bunch of our other friends were already there, so we said hi to them and pretty much ignored Sam. It's impossible to ignore him completely, because he takes over practice like he's the coach. Just because his brother Mike is a big star, he thinks that makes him the basketball expert of the world.

"OK, guys, let's get organized," he yelled. I was surprised he didn't pull out a whistle. "We need to practice free throws. Line up at the free throw line and we'll take turns. Three shots per man."

Zack and I lined up behind Tony Anzaldi and Luis Ramez. They are both cool guys and good players who don't brag and act like you-know-who. Both of them sank one out of three. Zack scored zip, but he just shrugged and went to the end of the line. Then it was my turn.

My hands were sweaty as I took the ball from Zack. I dribbled a few times, aimed, and threw. Bingo! A sinker. I grinned at Zack at the end of the line, aimed, and threw again. The ball rolled around the rim for half a second. Then it hit the ground without going through the hoop. I frowned and didn't look at Sam. I knew he'd try to throw me off. I licked my lips, dribbled, screwed up my face and aimed again. Another miss.

"That's what happens when you're too interested in girls!" Sam hollered. "Next!"

I shot him a dirty look and went to the end of the line. I was never going to live down writing on Trish's Riley's back. I could see that as plain as cheese pizza. My mind shifted to the dog.

But then something told me to turn around. I did and there was Trish at the fence by the pool waving her green and white pompons at me. Green and white are the colors of the Pinecrest Flying Eagles. I pretended like I didn't see her, but just knowing she was there messed up my concentration.

The next time my turn came up it was even worse. It was like I had forgotten everything I had ever known about basketball. I missed all three shots. One of them was so bad I don't even want to talk about it. Let's just say it's a good thing it wasn't tryouts. If the coach had seen that bomb, he wouldn't even let me sell popcorn at the snack bar, much less be on the team.

As soon as we finished shooting baskets, we switched to speed dribbling, which was a little better—as long as you don't count the time I lost control of the ball and rammed it into a tree. I kept telling myself to concentrate, but all I could think of was the dog.

"You got time to go somewhere?" I asked Zack when we finally wrapped it up for the day.

"Can't," he said. "We're having company for supper. Some people my dad used to know are in town. Where do you want to go anyway?" He pulled his bike out from the heap of bikes on the grass and looked at me with interest. Zack is always ready for a new adventure. That's one of the reasons I like him so much.

"I'm going to stop in at Dr. Barry's animal hospital and visit the dog. Do you think they'll let me see him?" I asked, pulling my bike out too.

Before he could answer, Trish Riley came over to the edge of the basketball court. "Hey, Mickey!" she called. "Come here. I've got something to tell you. It's important."

Quickly, I looked over my shoulder to see if Sam was watching. He was talking to a bunch of his buddies, but I didn't want to risk him seeing Trish and me talking. "Can't," I told her. "I've got to get somewhere." Which was sort of true. The animal hospital would be closing soon and I had to be home in time for supper.

I hopped on my bike and headed down the

street. "See ya!" I hollered over my shoulder. I really said it to Zack, but it kind of included Trish too.

Dr. Barry's animal hospital is on Wooster Street, not too far from my house. Of course, that's the one street I'm not supposed to cross. But since I didn't have to cross it to get to the hospital, I figured the Wooster Street Rule didn't matter. Especially since this was sort of an emergency.

I parked my bike in front of the animal hospital and went in. Right away I was blasted with a medicine smell, mixed with the smell of animals and the kind of cleaner they use in people hospitals.

"Hi. My name is Mickey McGhee," I told the lady at the counter. She had long fingernails like bird claws decorated with red, white, and blue stripes. It looked like she'd stopped by the auto body shop for a paint job on her way to work. "Yesterday a puppy got run over by a car at the church and Dr. Barry did surgery on him. Do you think I could maybe visit him?" I asked.

The lady with the claws sighed. She got up from her computer and disappeared into the back room. Pretty soon Dr. Barry came to the door that leads back to the examining rooms.

"Hi, Mickey," she greeted me. "Here to see the dog? That's OK, but I have to warn you, he's been having a tough time."

A tough time? What was she talking about? He'd made it through surgery just fine. My mom said so. I was confused, but I nodded and walked past her into the back. Rows of cages lined two walls. I stopped under the bright lights and looked around. Most of the animals were either sleeping or lying quietly—except for two big dogs that were howling at each other like coyotes. It was pretty funny, but I didn't laugh because almost right away I spotted *my* dog.

"Oh, wow," I breathed, going over to his cage. I was shocked. His stomach was covered with bandages and his back leg was in a cast. He was lying so still he looked like a statue, except that his tiny chest was going up and down real hard like mine does after a close game. Tears burned my eyes, but I tried not to let them show.

"He doesn't look too good," I said in a small voice. "He's not going to—he wouldn't ..." I couldn't bring myself to say the word "die" out loud.

"I don't know yet, Mickey," Dr. Barry said quietly. "He's very, very sick, but I promise I'm going to keep doing everything I can to help him."

I nodded. I wanted to thank her, but the words wouldn't come out. If I didn't swallow the lump in my throat right then, I knew I'd burst into tears.

Dr. Barry gave my shoulders a squeeze like she understood how I felt. I bet she did too. Dr. Barry is a good vet. She takes care of animals without worrying about how much money she's going to get.

To my surprise, she opened the door of his cage. "See, Mickey?" she said, gently stroking the puppy's head. "You can pet him a little. I think he'd like that. One of the best things we can do right now is show him how much we want him to live."

I reached out and touched his soft, fuzzy, little head. I would stand there petting him all day and all night, if it would make him want to get better.

Already a prayer was forming in my head. My mom always says you don't have to beg God for things. You just have to ask Him and trust that He will do what's best. But this time I begged. I pleaded with Him not to let my dog die before he got a chance to hang out with Zack and me. I could just see the three of us running around the concrete pad shooting baskets. One! Two! Three! Every last shot a sinker and the dog barking like crazy.

Dr. Barry went into a little room off to the side and left us alone. I looked into the puppy's eyes, then brought my face down close by his. "You've got to hang in there, little guy," I whispered into the long, shaggy hair by his ears.

"You and I belong together. Yeah. That's right. You're going to come to live at my house. You'll like it. I've got a sister named Meggie, and a mom, and a dad. We're going to have a great old time. When I make the team you'll be able to come to practice and everything. But you have to get better, OK?"

I lifted my head and stroked his ear with one finger. The dog gave me a look I can't describe. I mean, I can, but it's kind of embarrassing. Let's just say that two big tears plopped out of my eyes and landed on the puppy's head. And right then I didn't even care who saw!

6

Dog Gone

"Mickey!" Zack yelled out the window of the bus the next morning. "Hurry up! I've got big news!"

The door to the bus was jammed with kids. A third grader had dropped the log cabin he'd made for social studies. Smashed pretzels and cracked white icing mortar lay scattered across the steps like gravel in a parking lot.

"What?" I hollered back.

"Can't tell you! Wait till you get here!"

If Zack wouldn't even say what kind of news it was, it had to be worth waiting for. I hopped first on one foot and then on the other. By the time the pretzel mess was finally cleaned up, I felt like I was going to hop out of my skin.

"It's about the dog," Zack said when I flopped down beside him on the cracked black seat.

"The dog?"

"Yeah. The one that got run over." He looked over his shoulder to see if anyone was listening. Zack's so tall he can see over the top of the seat without having to stand up. "It's not the only one."

I frowned. "You mean another dog got run over too?"

"No!" He looked over his shoulder again and lowered his voice. "I mean it's not the only dog. There are two more of them from the same litter. I found them yesterday on the way home. They were by the bushes near where we found the hurt one."

I didn't get it. I mean it was cool that there were more dogs, but I couldn't see why he was acting like he was sharing FBI secrets by telling me about them. I must have looked confused, because right away he said, "Don't you get it? Somebody must have dumped them off. If we don't say anything about them, we can each get one. My dad already said I could."

Right away I thought of the puppy lying alone in his cage at Dr. Barry's animal hospital and shook my head. "No way," I said. "I already have a dog."

Zack's eyes widened. "You mean the hurt one? But, Mickey, he's the runt of the litter. The other two are way bigger. That's probably why they got out of the way when that car went tearing through there. They're healthy. That one …" He let his voice trail off.

Behind me I could hear Sam Sherman's buddies laughing. They were doing what they do every morning—making fun of a guy in our class named Ernie Crain. They call him "Crainiac, the Brainiac," because he's so smart and can read on a seventh-grade level. He always acts like he can't hear them, but I know how it makes him feel.

A terrible thought wormed its way into my brain. If those guys saw me with some itty-bitty little dog, they'd laugh themselves silly! Especially if I made the team and had to hang out with them all the time. Maybe I'd better take a bigger one while I had the chance.

"I don't care," I said out loud. "I want him." But the truth was, I wasn't so sure I did anymore. I shook my head to rid myself of the thought.

"OK," Zack agreed. He sounded like he couldn't believe it. "Maybe Trish Riley will take the other big one then."

I didn't say anything. The terrible thought had crept back into my head as quiet as a cat burglar. I loved that little dog. I didn't care if he was the runt of the litter. But I couldn't stand the thought of them teasing me any more than they already did.

The rest of the way to school I didn't say much. Later, on the playground, I got Zack to ask Trish if she wanted the other big dog. Partly it was because I didn't want Sam to see me talking to her, but mostly it was because I didn't want to hear her answer.

"She's going to meet us at the church after school," Zack reported after talking to Trish by the swings. "She thinks she might be able to take it, but she has to ask first."

The terrible thought wiggled into my brain again. Maybe Trish would like the little dog better. After all, he was the runt and Trish was a girlie kind of girl.

If Trish took him, he'd have a good home. I'd still be able to see him whenever I wanted, because he'd live right down the street from me. It was a good idea. It was a great idea, except that it made me feel lower than an earthworm.

After school Zack and I rode over to the church as fast as we could. It had rained in the afternoon, so the sidewalk was slick enough to slow us down. We hung a right and headed up the drive to the parking lot behind the Sunday school rooms.

"Zack!" I cried, jamming on my brakes suddenly. "Look!"

Behind me, Zack slammed on his brakes too and skidded to a stop. "What?"

I pointed to a black and silver bike standing by itself in the middle of the empty lot. "What's that doing back there?"

Zack's jaw dropped open. We looked around for some sign of Trish, but there wasn't any. "What do we do now?" he asked.

"We get to the bottom of this," I said, pedaling hard toward the parking lot. I was so mad I could feel my heart pounding in my ears. I spotted the bike's owner crawling around on the grass at the edge of the concrete. All you could see was the lower half of him sticking out from under a bright red bush, but I knew exactly who it was and what he was after.

"Hey!" I hollered. "What do you think you're doing?"

Sam Sherman sat up on his heels and looked at us. He was holding a mostly brown puppy with one tan ear. "Getting myself a dog. What's it look like I'm doing, Shrimpo?" he demanded. His voice had a mean edge to it, one I'd never heard before.

"Who told you that dog was here?" I demanded. I sounded tough, but inside I was starting to feel uneasy. Usually Sam sounds braggy or teasing. This time he sounded like he was aiming for a fight.

He stood up and came closer, carrying the squirming pup against his chest. "I have my ways," he said, sticking out his chin. "What's it to you?"

I looked at Zack, but Zack just shrugged. I knew he was telling me to back off. I wasn't about to get into a fight with Sam Sherman. Fighting is a stupid way to handle stuff. Besides, I knew he could make Cream of Wheat out of me, and probably out of Zack too. Zack may be tall, but he's not the toughest guy you'd ever want to meet.

I ignored Sam's question. Getting those dogs meant everything to me. Sam Sherman already had a dog. He also had a brother who was a basketball star, and Sam would probably end up playing center on the team. It was no fair that he should get another dog on top of all that, when I didn't know if I'd even *make* the team for sure.

"Where's the other dog?" I demanded. "There's supposed to be two dogs." I wasn't sure I should say this, in case he'd take them both. But I had to know if the other one was still around. I glared at Sam, but didn't make a move toward him. Zack did the same.

Sam shrugged. Now that he saw we weren't going to try and stop him, he seemed like himself again. He walked over to his bike and opened the door to a pet carrier strapped to the back. I had been so surprised to see his bike in the lot, I hadn't noticed the carrier before. The puppy struggled as Sam shoved it inside the red plastic box and slammed the wire door.

"If you can find it, you can have it," he said, getting on his bike. "See ya."

Zack and I watched as he rode off towards Adams Street with the puppy yelping in the box behind him. Now there was only one dog. That is, if we could find it. And three people wanted it. Of course, there was also the runt. One of us could still have *him*.

A picture flashed in my mind of his sad, brown puppy eyes looking at me that night at the hospital. He needed me, and I'd told him he was coming to live at my house. I felt sick, like Sam had punched me in the stomach.

"How did *that* happen?" Zack demanded as Sam disappeared from sight. Zack parked his bike and headed over to the grassy area around the edges of the lot. He yanked open a big, green, prickly bush from the middle and looked inside. "Do you think one of his spies heard us talking on the bus?" he asked, shaking his head. "I was so careful to be quiet."

"No way they could have heard us," I replied. "Sam must have been over here and seen the dogs or something." I got down on my knees and started helping Zack look for the last puppy. The ground under the bushes was damp. Wetness soaked through the knees of my jeans, but I didn't care.

"What are we going to do now?" I asked from under the red bush. "I mean if we find him, who gets him?"

Zack stopped searching and brushed his thick, dark hair off his forehead with the back of a muddy hand. He looked like he'd never thought about it until this second. "Oh, wow! You're right. I sort of forgot I'd promised one to Trish." For a second he was quiet. Then he sighed and said, "Looks like you made the right choice after all, sticking with the runt, Mick."

The words sent a hot flush creeping up my neck. Zack didn't know about my terrible thought. All he knew was that I had wound up with a dog and he might not get one.

"Yeah," I agreed, crawling clear to the other end of the bushes. I didn't want to talk about it. Nobody could argue that the runt wasn't mine. Nobody. But I felt like a total creep.

We were still looking for the last puppy when Trish pulled up on her pink and purple bike. "Sorry I'm late, guys," she called, coming over to join us. She had on a Cleveland Indians cap. It was navy blue with the red and white Chief Wahoo on the front. "Did you find the puppies?"

"Not yet," I replied looking at Zack. "There's only one left anyway. Sam Sherman got the other one before we got here."

Trish's blue eyes popped. "Sam?" she yelled. "Sam Sherman got one of those dogs? No! He can't ..."

"Aw, forget Sam," Zack said, cutting her off. "The important thing is to find the other dog. Unless Sam and his pals already got him."

"NO!" Trish cried. Her voice came out so loud, it made me jump. "He can't have them! No! We have to get them back!" She took off her baseball cap and ran her hands through her curly brown hair like she wanted to pull it out of her head.

I had never seen Trish Riley this worked up. "We have to get them back!" she screamed. To my surprise, tears puddled up in her eyes. Trish may be a girlie kind of girl, but she almost never cries.

"We can't," Zack said again. "He got here first. All we can do is try to find the other one. Sam was ready to fight for that dog."

Trish ignored Zack and turned to me. "Mickey, ..." she began.

But I shook my head. "Zack's right, Trish. There's nothing we can do."

Trish didn't say anything. The tears were ready to spill out of her eyes. She wiped them on the sleeve of her pink jacket and ran toward the back of the parking lot. "Here, puppy, puppy, puppy," she called, waving her Indians cap. "Here, puppy!"

Not even a leaf moved. The parking lot was as quiet as the inside of the empty church.

"Here, puppy!" Trish called again. "Here, puppy!"

Nothing happened. The dog was gone.

7

Two Clues and a Big Surprise

"I need to go to the animal hospital," I told Zack the next day after school. "I'm skipping practice."

Zack stared at me like I'd just said I was quitting b-ball forever. "But, Mickey, tryouts are Saturday," he reminded me. "We only have two more days to get in shape."

I knew that, just like I knew I hadn't been practicing enough. But what was I supposed to do? It wasn't *my* fault there were sick and missing dogs to worry about.

For a half of a second, panic shot through me like a lightning bolt. Maybe I'd goofed off so much, it would cost me a spot on the team. That thought shook me up. But the thought of the dog sick and alone at the hospital, shook me up even more. I'd tried to pray about my mixed-up feelings about him, but the guilty feeling kept getting in the way.

The minute I got home I asked Mom if I could visit the puppy. She handed me a stack of co-op cookies and said OK. She even let me ride my bike over, as long as I followed the Wooster Street Rule. I stuffed the cookies into my pocket and tore out the door before she could change her mind.

At the animal hospital, the lady at the front desk waved her striped claws at the door and told me to go on back.

"Hi, Mickey," Dr. Barry greeted me as I came into the room where the cages were. She was giving a cat a shot. She stuck a needle into its fat black neck. "Guess what? I've got good news!" She pulled the needle out and patted the cat on the head. It blinked at her, but never moved a muscle.

"Your young friend is looking much better today," she said when I didn't say anything. "He sure is a little scrapper!"

"Really? He's better?" My heart leaped in my chest as I went over to the puppy's cage. He was still bandaged, but his eyes were bright and alert. The second he saw me, his bushy, little tail thumped on the floor of the cage. He knew who I was! No doubt about it!

"When do you think he can get out of here?" I asked, poking my finger through the wire cage. He stuck out his little, pink tongue and began to lick it.

"In a week or so," Dr. Barry replied. "We're planning to return him to the Humane Society for adoption." She came over to stand beside me. "Unless, of course, *you* want him, Mickey. If anyone deserves this dog, it's you."

She wouldn't be saying that if she knew the truth. I didn't know which was worse—her words or the puppy's thumping tail. All of a sudden, they both made me mad. It was like everybody was yanking at my sleeve, wanting something. Ever since the dog got run over and Zack found the puppies, it was like I didn't have a life anymore. All I thought about were dogs, dogs, dogs, and now I might not even make the team because I'd spent so much worrying about them all. I mumbled something about having to ask my mom.

Outside, I checked the clock in the window of the fireplace store. It was early. The guys would still be at the park working out. Maybe if I hurried, I could still get in a little practice.

I jumped on my bike and sped over to Pinecrest. It was time to quit thinking about dogs, and start thinking about tryouts, I told myself. There were only two more days and I had a lot of catching up to do. I wheeled into the parking lot and spotted Sam Sherman first thing. He was wearing his brother's red number 36 shirt again. It still looked like a dress.

"Hey, Mickey!" Zack called when he saw me. "You're just in time. We're practicing dribbling."

I ignored Sam and got at the end of the line behind Zack. The whole time I waited for my turn, I watched Sam screaming orders and acting important. The more I watched, the madder I got. He had done something with that other dog. I was sure of it.

By the time it was my turn, I felt like a can of soda shaken until it was ready to explode.

Grabbing the ball from Zack, I slammed it down hard on the concrete court. The dull, angry thud filled me with power. Slam! I beat it down again. I did it a couple more times. And then, I took off running with it. Down the court and back up I dashed, slamming that ball harder than I ever had in my life.

"Look at Mickey!"

"Wow! Check it out!"

All around me I could hear the guys hollering. Blood coursed through my body faster than a race car on a speedway. I was on fire. But when I tossed the ball into the basket, it grazed the rim and rolled away before I could recover it.

"Next! Next!" Sam Sherman hollered. "Quit hogging the court, McGhee!"

I tossed the ball to LaMar Watson and ran to the end of the line. My face was as red as the cherry on a sundae. It didn't make any sense. I was so charged, so pumped, and I *still* couldn't sink a decent basket. How was I ever going to make the team at this rate? Just because I wanted a dog, did that mean I couldn't be on the team too? Did God want me to choose one thing or the other? I was already trying to choose between dogs.

After practice, Zack and I rode home together. I told him the good news about the puppy, but I didn't say anything about Dr. Barry wanting me to adopt it. I also didn't say anything about how scared I was that I'd blown my chance to make the team. Instead, I reached into my pocket and pulled out two leftover cookies. Both of them were broken. I pulled up alongside Zack and gave him a big chunk of one of them.

"Thanks," he said, stuffing the whole thing into his mouth. He mumbled something through the crumbs. I didn't hear what it was, because just then Trish Riley honked the horn on her pink and purple bike.

"Hey, guys, wait up!" she hollered from behind us. "I need to tell you something."

Zack and I looked at each other and shrugged. We might as well listen since none of the guys were around. We hopped off our bikes and waited for her to catch up.

Trish braked hard and stopped, but didn't get

off her bike. "Um, uh …" she began, tugging on the brim of her baseball cap. It was a red one today with little white dots on it.

We waited for her to go on.

"The thing is, …" she began, still tugging on the cap, "The thing is, I have to tell you something, but …"

Zack and I got back on our bikes. This showed signs of being embarrassing. If she told me she liked me in front of Zack, I would croak right there in the middle of Arvin Avenue! As a matter of fact, if she told me she liked me in front of *me*, I'd croak! I felt crummy enough for one day, without adding any mushy stuff to it.

"Just be careful," she blurted finally. "And think about the number 36 and the color red."

Our mouths dropped open. Before we could say anything, she sped past us toward her house. For a second we stood astride our bikes on the sidewalk, staring at each other. Finally Zack said, "What was that all about?"

I smoothed down the hair sticking up on the top of my head. (I call that my "stick-up" hair.) "I don't know," I said slowly. "But Sam's brother's basketball shirt is red, and his number is 36. Is Trish trying to tell us Sam did something? We already know he took one dog and maybe two."

"Nah." Zack shook his head. "That doesn't

make any sense. Why wouldn't she just come out and say it, if she thought he did something like that? Why would she have to act so weird? She doesn't like Sam Sherman any better than we do."

I thought about how Sam had been so ready to fight that day in the church parking lot. He was a big guy and he liked to pick on people. "Maybe she's scared," I said.

"*Scared*?" Zack squawked. "Why would she be …"

The sudden squeal of tires behind us drowned out Zack's words. We turned around just in time to see a red flash of car zoom up Wooster Street. We were too slow to see who was in it, but it looked like it had taken the corner on two wheels.

"Crazy drivers," I muttered. And then it hit me. "ZACK!" I screamed. "That was the car that ran over the dog at the church!"

"You bet it was!" Zack agreed. "I'd know it anywhere."

There was no way we could chase it on our bikes, especially since it had a huge head start. "What should we do?" I asked.

"Nothing we *can* do," Zack said, starting to pedal again. "We just have to keep our eyes open in case we see it again."

I put my feet on the pedals of my bike, bore down, and followed his wobbly path up the street.

My mind was whirring faster than an electric fan in August. Now there were four things we couldn't figure out:

Who owned the flashy, red car?

What was Trish trying to tell us?

Why had she acted so weird?

And what had Sam Sherman done with the missing dog?

Of course, that didn't even count the two big things I had to figure out for myself: What was I going to do about the puppy at Dr. Barry's animal hospital? And how was I going to make up for all the time I hadn't spent practicing for the team?

Up ahead, I could see my little sister Meggie outside in front of our house wearing her pink bunny slippers and a Superman cape. The second she spotted me, she came tearing down the street toward us waving her arms. "Mickey! Hurry!" she hollered. "Mama brought a surprise!"

"I'm coming!" I snapped. I knew I wasn't being nice, but she can be so embarrassing sometimes. The red cape billowed out behind her like a sheet on a clothesline. It was part of an old Halloween costume I'd worn in kindergarten. The closer she got, the better I could see that both of her eyelids were covered with some kind of glittery blue gunk.

"Hurry, Mickey! It's the best surprise in the

whole *world!*" she screamed, jumping up and down beside me.

Zack laughed. "See ya later, Mick," he called as I swerved into my driveway.

I didn't care about any surprise. Mom had probably just ordered a pizza for dinner. Most days the thought of steamy cheese and pepperoni would have lit a fire under me, but not today. I felt grouchy. Why did Mom let Meggie run around in stupid clothes and eye gunk, anyway?

I took my time putting my bike away. Then I walked slowly up the driveway toward the house. Meggie was holding the screen door on the side of the house, waiting for me. Sighing, I climbed the steps, and went past her inside and up the few steps to the kitchen. I sniffed. It sure didn't smell like pizza.

In fact, it smelled exactly like …

A brown blur raced around the corner from the living room and flung itself at me. I stepped back to keep from getting knocked over and blinked hard. I couldn't believe my eyes! It smelled exactly like what it was. Dog! The very same dog Sam Sherman had carried away in the red pet carrier.

8

Something in the Glass

"Wh-where did he come from?" I sputtered.

Mom beamed at me brighter than Christmas morning. "A nice young man brought him into the shelter this afternoon," she said, smoothing down my stick-up hair. "I took one look at him, and knew he was the one we've been waiting for. Do you like him, Mickey?"

I nodded and tried to say something. The words stuck in my throat. I reached down and scratched the dog's ears. He let out a few little yips and tried to leap into my arms. Meggie squealed and jumped up and down, clapping her hands.

"Isn't he cute?" Mom asked, laughing as I dodged wet puppy kisses. "He even has a little sister. She looks just like him, except that she has more tan on her ears. If you want, we can go down to the shelter and take a look at her tomorrow, and you can make a trade." She stopped and stared at me. "What's wrong, Mickey? You haven't said a word."

My mouth was hanging open. My eyes were bugging out. My mouth felt stiff as cardboard. Both of the dogs Zack and I were looking for had ended up at the shelter. And now one of them was right here in our very own kitchen. I couldn't wait to tell Zack!

"Nothing's wrong," I said, quickly. "He's great! Thanks, Mom. I've got to call Zack!"

I ran to the phone and dialed Zack's number with the puppy yipping at my heels. "Zack!" I shouted when he answered. "You aren't going to believe what just happened!"

By the time I finished telling him, Zack was so excited, he was shouting back at me. "This is so cool!" he screamed in my ear. "Now we can each have a dog, after all. There's one for you, one for me, and one for Trish."

That stopped me short. The little dog was racing around trying to catch the phone cord between his teeth. I watched him and thought about the puppy at Dr. Barry's. Mom had given me this dog. If I gave him to Zack and took the runty one for myself, it would make her feel bad. Wouldn't it?

"Yeah," I said. "We've got three all right. I was thinking that maybe you'd like that one down at the shelter. Mom says she's pretty cute. What do you think?" I held my breath.

Zack took a long time to reply. "Yeah, sure," he said finally. "We can go get her after tryouts on Saturday."

He didn't want the girl dog. He wanted the one I had. His voice had said it all. Who was I kidding? Mom wouldn't care which dog I ended up owning. She'd already offered to make a trade. I was using her as an excuse, so I could hang onto this dog until I decided what to do about the one at Dr. Barry's.

Back in the kitchen, Meggie and Mom were filling a bowl with dog food. I stood in the doorway and watched. The new puppy was big and sturdy with huge paws. Compared to him, the one at Dr. Barry's looked like a hamster. I couldn't show up at the park with such a measly little dog. The guys would howl. It's different for Zack. He's almost as big as Sam Sherman. He could get away with owning a runt or a girl dog, and nobody would say a thing.

Weird as it sounds, that cheered me up. Nobody could blame me if I kept the dog I had and gave the girl dog to Zack and the runt to Trish. Nobody.

The next morning my eyes opened before Mom came upstairs. It was the last day before tryouts! My feet hit the floor faster than it takes the shot clock to run out at a basketball game. I had to get in some serious practice today to make up for lost time. The puppy was already in the kitchen with Mom and Meggie when I went down to breakfast.

"Mickey, look!" Meggie shouted. "The puppy brought one of your socks upstairs in his teeth." She picked up a smelly gym sock that had been in the dirty clothes pile on the basement floor and held it by the toe. "Eeeeeew. He must really like you." She wrinkled her nose and made a face.

The puppy ran over to me as if he agreed. He was a great dog. Maybe I'd call him "Shaq" after Shaquille O'Neal. Or "Magic" after Magic Johnson.

I grabbed a piece of toast, ate two bites, and hurried outside to shoot a few hoops before school. It was cold and as quiet as night on Arvin Avenue. The sun wasn't fully up yet, so the air was gray and misty. I took a deep breath and let it out, watching it float away like a cloud.

I still hadn't practiced passing much, but there wasn't anything I could do about that by myself. The next most important thing was my jump shot. It looks easy on TV, but it's not. You have to remember not to release the ball until you're at the very top of the jump. Sometimes when I'm moving really fast, I let go too soon.

I ran in place to warm up for awhile and then

did some jumping jacks. They made me feel sort of stupid, but there was nobody outside to see. Then I started dribbling. *Thud! Thud! Thud!* The sound of the ball slapping the fresh concrete sent a surge of power to my muscles.

I ran to the basket, bent my knees, and spread my fingers to support the ball from behind. Then I pointed the elbow of my shooting arm toward the basket and leaped straight up. My feet were a shoulder's width apart, just like they were supposed to be. Arcing the ball toward the basket, I let go and came down hard on the soles of my sneakers. The ball hit the backboard and bounced off.

Huh? I stared at the ball as it rolled into the rosebush by the side door. What had happened? I did everything right, and it still hadn't gone in. My heart pounded. I tried the shot again and again. Each time was the same. I couldn't sink a ball, no matter how hard I tried.

"Mickey! It's getting late. You need to comb your hair and gather up your school things," Mom called out the kitchen window.

"Aw, Mom, I just got out here!" I complained.

But she'd already closed the window. I went into the house and walked by the puppy without even stopping to play with him. I was in deep trouble. The jump shot had never been my best thing, but I'd always managed to land at least a couple. Now I couldn't land even one. Something was wrong, and I didn't have a clue what it was.

After school I caught up with Zack by the bus. He had been quiet all day, like he was sort of mad at me. "Want to get in some practice at my house tonight?" I asked, getting in line behind him.

He shook his head. "Can't. I promised Luis and Tony I'd practice with them."

I waited for him to invite me to join them. "Where you guys going?" I asked finally, when it was clear he wasn't going to. "To the park? I thought Sam said no practice today."

"He did," Zack replied. He shifted his backpack and climbed up the steps to the bus.

Inside, he grabbed a seat next to Luis and left me to find one of my own. I slumped down next to Jim Callen, one of Sam Sherman's closest friends. It was the only seat left that wasn't next to a girl.

"Hey, Shrimpo," Callen said, nudging me in the ribs with his elbow. "Where's your best buddy?"

I ignored the question and stared miserably at the back of Zack's head. I knew why Zack was mad, and part of me didn't blame him, but another part did. Zack knew how bad I got teased. He also knew that if it hadn't been for my mother, we'd never have known about the dogs being at the shelter in the first place. He was being a total creep about the whole thing. He was lucky I was giving him any dog at all!

Callen leaned across me to talk to his friends across the aisle. "McGhee's so short he shoots baskets with the ball Trish Riley uses to play jacks!" he told them.

I turned my head and stared out the window. They snorted.

"McGhee's so little his basketball shoes are made by Baby-Bok!" one of them snickered.

"Hey, I've got one!" somebody hollered from behind me. "McGhee's so short that if he makes the team, the coach will have to give him a single number. His back's too skinny for two."

One-liners flew around my ears like spitballs. I slumped down lower in my seat and tried to ignore them. But my face was redder than the flashy car that had run over the puppy in the church parking lot.

At home I dumped my backpack on the steps by the basement door and ran to the garage for my ball. I'd show those jerks a thing or two about basketball. Tomorrow they wouldn't be laughing. When I landed a spot on the team, they'd know I'm just as good as they are. For a few seconds I circled around the pad, dribbling the ball and letting the anger fire up my muscles. But it didn't work. Even before my feet left the ground, I knew my jump shot was just as lousy as it had been that morning.

"Hi, Mickey!" a voice called behind me.

I grabbed the ball after it bounced off the backboard and covered my face with it. The last person on earth I wanted to talk to was coming up my driveway on a pink and purple bike.

"Hi, Trish. I'm kind of busy right now," I said, not looking at her. I aimed the ball, squinted, and pictured the follow-through in my head.

"I know," she said. "Tomorrow's tryouts. But I just wanted to ask you when I can get my dog. Zack says you're giving me one. Which one is it, Mickey? Is it the big one your Mom brought home? Can I see him? Please? Just a peak? I won't stay long. I promise."

Blood rushed to my face. What was I supposed to say? I didn't know which dog I was giving her. "I can't right now. He's—uh—sleeping," I muttered. My face was as red as ketchup.

Trish tugged on her bright yellow baseball cap and glared at me. "That's a big fat lie, Mickey McGhee, and you know it," she said.

She was right. It *was* a lie. And I *did* know it. I was already sorry I'd told it. "Look, Trish, I've got to go somewhere right now," I said miserably.

"I don't have time to show you the dog, but you are definitely getting one."

"When?" she demanded.

I looked up at the kitchen window. Inside the house I could hear the dog barking and Meggie laughing. "Tomorrow," I replied. "After tryouts."

Trish brightened. "Great! I'll see you then, Mickey!" She turned her bike around and headed back down the drive. At the bottom she hollered, "Good luck tomorrow!"

I watched her go, feeling flatter than a deflated ball. Between the dogs and tryouts, tomorrow was shaping up to be the worst day of my life. I looked up at the dull gray sky and said a prayer out loud. It only had three words. "Help me, God."

As soon as the prayer was out of my heart, a weird thing happened. I felt as charged up as a brand new battery. I can't explain it, but suddenly I knew I needed to go to Dr. Barry's. I had no idea what I was going to do when I got there, but something inside me just said, "Go!"

I ran in the house and asked Mom if I could ride over. To my surprise, she said OK right away, and she didn't even mention the Wooster Street Rule.

I pedaled hard down Arvin Avenue and took the corner fast. Whatever was sending me on this trip, kept saying, "Go, Mickey! Go!" On Wooster Street I screeched to a stop in front of the animal hospital and hopped off my bike. My heart was pounding as I pushed open the plate glass door. I started to go in, when I saw something reflected in the glass. It stopped me cold.

The flashy, red car that had run over the puppy was parked across the street!

Taking a Shot

For what seemed like an hour, I stood in the doorway feeling stupid. People came and went from the animal hospital, and I just kept standing there blocking their way. Finally, I walked to the edge of the curb and squinted my eyes. The license plate on the flashy, red car was too far away to read.

The only thing to do was to cross Wooster Street. But that meant I'd either have to leave my bike on the sidewalk by Dr. Barry's, or walk it across four lanes of traffic. I decided to leave it. If anybody tried to swipe it, I'd see them and do my Tarzan yell.

I ran across Wooster and down the sidewalk toward the car. Even before I reached it, I saw that the first part of the license plate exactly matched what Zack had told us! But then I thought of something. The owner was a hit and run driver. Maybe he was a hardened criminal too. He might try to mug me or kidnap me and hold me hostage for a million dollars. No way did my mom and dad have that kind of money. I ducked into the doorway of the hardware store and started plotting my escape.

Before I could work it out though, a tall skinny guy ran across Wooster Street and unlocked the driver's side door of the flashy, red car. He had come out of Dr. Barry's animal hospital! I was sure of it.

"Hey!" I hollered, hurrying over to the car. So much for escape plans.

The guy looked up from the door lock. "You talking to me?" he asked.

"I want to know why you ran over that dog at the church and just drove off," I said. Even while I was saying it, I knew it was a stupid thing to blurt out.

The guy straightened up and came around to the curb. I backed up a few paces toward the hardware store.

"How do you know about that?" he demanded.

I swallowed hard and wondered whether I should run or wait until I got an answer. I held my ground and stared him straight in the eye. He looked to be about 20 or so, and as tall as a giraffe.

"Never mind that," I replied, sounding braver than I felt. "I want to know why you did it, and why you just came out of Dr. Barry's hospital."

The guy leaned against the side of the car. He folded his arms across his chest and stared at me. I had the weird feeling I ought to know who he was, but I didn't.

"Look, kid," he said, "I don't know who you are, or why I'm bothering to tell you this, but here's the deal. I did run over the dog. But I didn't know it was a dog at the time. When I found out, I went over there to see how he was doing." He jabbed his thumb across the street toward Dr. Barry's.

"Oh." I mumbled. Another dumb thing to say. My mind was reeling. It was nice of him to care enough to go visit my—I mean *the*—dog, but I still wasn't sure I trusted him. "How did you find out it was a dog you hit?" I asked finally.

He looked at his watch and shrugged. "Somebody told me, OK? Look, it's been nice talkin' to you, kid, but I'm running late." He loped around to the driver's side of the car, got in, and started the engine.

"Hey, wait!" I hollered. But it was no use. He pulled out into traffic and roared down Wooster Street.

For a second I stared after him. I still felt like I ought to know him from somewhere. I scratched my head and tried to think. Then I remembered my bike, and ran across Wooster before the light changed. I climbed on, figuring I'd ride over to the park and see if Zack and the guys were there. Zack would never be able to stay mad at me when he heard this! But right away, I changed my mind, got off, and went inside the animal hospital.

The lady at the front desk was on the phone. I walked past her and pulled open the door to the back. I nearly bumped into Dr. Barry.

"Mickey!" she exclaimed, her hands full of folders. "You scared me!"

"Sorry," I apologized. Over her shoulder I could already see the puppy. He saw me too and let out a sharp little bark.

"Sounds like somebody's happy to see you," Dr. Barry said, laughing. "He sure is getting popular. You're his second visitor this afternoon."

"You mean that guy who was just here?" I asked, walking over to the cage. My heart picked up speed. "He's the one who ran over him." I waited to see what Dr. Barry would say about that.

"That's true," she agreed. "He feels terrible about it too. That's why he took the rest of the dogs to the shelter."

"Well, you two visit. I've got a poodle with a broken leg to see."

She pushed through the door and left me

standing by the puppy's cage with my mouth shaped like a doughnut. The tall guy with the flashy car had taken the puppies to the shelter? But how, when Sam had them? Suddenly, I couldn't wait to get out of there. I patted the puppy's paws, told him I'd see him later, and beat it outside.

At the park there was no sign of Zack. I looked at the nearly empty basketball courts and felt the excitement drain out of me. A basketball somebody must have forgotten to take back to the rec center lay in the grass behind one of the baskets. I walked over, picked it up, and bounced it a few times on the concrete. I knew I needed to work on my jump shot. But I had no energy.

Zack and the rest of the guys had probably gone to Zack's house to practice. They would all make the team and I'd be left in the stands. And tomorrow I had to give Trish a dog.

I dribbled the ball again and made a pass at the basket. It missed. I tried another jump shot. That time it went in, but just barely. Maybe my feet weren't as wide apart as I thought they were. I jumped a few times and nearly tripped, trying to look down and see.

"Hey, kid!"

At the sound of the familiar voice, I whirled around. The tall guy with the flashy, red car was walking toward me.

"The problem's in your knees," he called. "The farther away from the basket you are, the deeper you have to bend them. Watch!"

He ran up alongside me, grabbed the ball, and took off. His jump shot was perfect.

"You're Mike Sherman," I said when he completed it. It wasn't a question. I was just stating what I suddenly knew. I'd never seen him play, because the State games are on cable and we only have regular TV. I'd never seen him around town either. But when he landed that basket, I knew in my bones, it had to be him.

"Yeah," he said. "You probably know my brother, Sam. He's trying out for the rec department team tomorrow. I came over to pick him up, but he isn't here."

"I know him. But I haven't seen him," I said. My mind felt like a whirling pinwheel. Mike Sherman, the guy everybody said would make the NBA next year, was standing right here in Pinecrest Park talking to *me*!

Mike looked at his watch and scowled. "I told him 5:00. He knows I have a date tonight."

I didn't know what to say to that, so I didn't say anything. I just stood there staring at him.

He scanned the park looking for Sam. Suddenly, he turned back to me and said, "Hey, if you want, I could help you with that jump shot while I wait."

"Uh—OK," I replied, stumbling over my words. "But, can I—uh—ask you something first?"

He nodded.

"How come you took the rest of the litter to the animal shelter?" I tilted back my head and looked up at him. Already my neck hurt from the stretch. "Those dogs belonged to Sam. He's the one who got them from the church."

Mike dribbled the ball. "Yeah, well," he said, dribbling even harder. Suddenly, he pivoted to the left and whipped around to face the backboard. As he turned, his right arm swept toward the basket. Snap! His wrists came forward. The ball rolled straight off his fingertips and into the hole. A perfect hook shot.

I watched in awe as he picked up the ball and came back to where I was standing. "You must be Mickey McGhee," he said.

I nodded.

He grinned, showing a mouthful of even, white teeth. "I thought so. I've been hearing a lot about you these days."

Yeah, I bet, I thought. But I didn't say anything.

"Sam talks about you all the time." He grinned at me again and I knew my hunch had been right.

Sam had not been telling him what a great guy I was.

"My brother had no business taking those dogs," he said. "I don't know why he did it, but it was wrong. We already have a dog, and he doesn't take all that good care of *him*. So I took the puppies to the shelter where they could get adopted."

"Th-thanks," I stuttered. "Th-that was great of you." I felt like a total dork, but I didn't know what else to say. Mike was nothing like Sam. He may not be all that great a driver, but he was a really nice guy, and the best college player in the *whole* state.

He laughed and pointed at the basket with a hand the size of a small pizza. "Look at the rim there," he told me. "At the back of it. Right in the middle. That's where you've got to aim if you want to land a jump shot. The idea isn't to throw AT the basket, but INTO it, right?"

"Right," I said taking the ball from him. I held it up and aimed it at the spot he showed me.

"OK, then," Mike coaxed. "Give it a try. Dribble, run, bend those knees and shoot. But keep your eye on the target. You can do it, buddy!"

I took off down the court like a rocket. Mike Sherman had called me buddy! Suddenly I had the energy of *two* guys. I aimed the ball at the back of the rim, bent my knees, and exploded into the air. The next seconds seemed like a freeze-frame from a movie. I hung in the air. The ball made a perfect arc. Then it sailed through the basket as smooth and easy as a candy bar falling down the shoot of a vending machine.

"Yessssssssssss!" I shouted, whirling around. "All righhhhhhht!" I was grinning like a jack o' lantern, until I spotted Sam Sherman standing beside his brother.

"Not bad, Shrimpo," Sam said, glaring at me. He turned to Mike, "Let's go."

"Not so fast," Mike told him. "I want to help Mickey a little more. You can play if you want to."

Sam stuck out his chin and glared at Mike. "I thought you were in such a big hurry," he accused. "If you're going to stay here and waste your time with Shrimpo, I'm going to the car."

"Your choice, little brother," Mike said mildly. "Want to try that again, Mickey?"

"Sure," I said. My eyes were the size of yo-yos as I watched Sam Sherman head for the parking lot with his head down.

Muggsy Bogues and the Underdogs

Coach Duffy shrilled his silver whistle. My stomach muscles clenched. This was it—tryouts.

"OK, guys, listen up!" Coach called. "I want you all to relax and have fun. This is a rec department program, so any boy who wants to play, plays. Of course, if you want to make the A-team, you're going to have to show me your best stuff."

For a split second my stomach went slack, but when he said "A-team" it balled up tighter than a fist. I wanted to make the A-team so bad I was shaking in my sneakers.

"I'm going to put you through a series of skill tests," Coach Duffy explained, looking us over. He caught my eye, looked away, and looked back. I knew what he was thinking. With Zack on one side and Luis Ramez on the other, I looked like an ant between two grasshoppers. My face turned redder than a ladybug's back.

"First we're going to do some exercises to warm up and then we'll start with dribbling. Ready?" Coach yelled.

"READY!" we shouted back.

All through the exercises, I pictured myself landing a perfect jump shot. By the time we got to the skill tests, I felt like I had fireworks exploding in my chest. When my turn came to dribble, I moved down the court like a cyclone. When we switched to shooting from the free-throw line, I sank two out of three. At shot blocking I was so fast and tricky that Luis Ramez started muttering in Spanish.

Coach Duffy blew his whistle. "OK! Let's see what you guys can do with jump shots!" he hollered. "Get going! We want to wrap this up and announce teams."

Fear washed over me like a hot shower. My palms were sweating as I took my place behind Luis. I wiped them on my shorts to keep them from dripping all over the court, but they kept on gushing. Trish Riley came in the door with her pompons. My heart sank as she tugged on her Indians baseball cap and gave me the thumbs-up sign. Pretty soon I was going to have to give her a dog and I still hadn't decided which one. But I'd worry about that later. Right now, I had to land a couple of jump shots.

God, I know Mom says to just tell you what I want and let YOU decide what's best for me. But this is an emergency! PLEASE God, just let me make A-

team starter, and I won't ask for anything else 'til Christmas!

Luis scored two out of three and passed me the ball. Everything Mike Sherman told me ran though my brain like e-mail messages flying across a computer screen. *Bend your knees deep. Keep your eye on the target. Point with your elbow. Keep your legs spread as wide as your shoulders. Don't let go of the ball until you reach the top of your jump.* I did every single thing he said.

And I missed.

I picked up the ball and walked slowly back to the start line.

"It's OK, Mick," Tony Anzaldi whispered. "You'll do it this time."

I screwed up my face, squinted my eyes and tried again. The ball hit the backboard and bounced off.

"That's what happens when you skip practice," Sam Sherman said loud enough for me to hear.

If I missed my third and last try, it was over. No A-team. No stardom. Maybe even no NBA. Coach Duffy would only remember that I was too shrimpy to sink a single jump shot. I wiped my hands on my shorts and aimed.

Please God. I know I haven't practiced as much as I should. And I know I've been a rat about the dogs, but …

The door to the rec center gym opened and Mike Sherman walked in. He saw me standing with the ball and broke into a grin. His hand came up and the thumb and pointer finger formed a little round "o." I couldn't believe it. Mike Sherman, future NBA player, was giving me the OK sign! After that all I cared about were the ball, the basket, and my body bursting through the air. Even before the shot sailed through the hoop I knew I'd landed it!

"Yay, Mickey!" Trish hollered, waving her pompons.

I walked over to the bleachers in a daze. Tony Anzaldi was up next, but I didn't watch. All I wanted to do was talk to Mike.

"Th-thanks," I stuttered when I got over to where he was sitting on the front bleacher. "I-I was in trouble out there. I missed the other two shots."

Mike grinned and ruffled my hair. "No problem. You landed that one like a pro."

I muttered an embarrassed thanks as Trish came running over, trailing little wisps of glossy green and white paper from her pompons. "Mickey! You did so good!" she cried. "Can I get my dog today?"

My head spun. She'd gone from "Congratulations" to "Can I have my dog?" with nothing in between. I heard my voice say, "Sure. How would you like a nice big, healthy girl dog? She's the one we couldn't find that day."

"Oooooooh, Mickey!" she squealed, dropping her pompons. Before I saw it coming, she threw her arms around my neck and gave me a hug. My face turned redder than a Valentine heart.

I shook myself free and stepped back. Trish grabbed my arm and pulled me aside. Now that she had the mushy stuff out of the way, she looked serious. "Do you know who you were talking to back there?" she whispered.

"Sure. Mike Sherman, Sam's brother," I said. "He's a nice guy. He ..."

Trish shook her head. "No, Mickey! He's not nice!" she hissed. "He's the one who ran over the dog. I saw him when I left the co-op after that lady told me to go home. Remember? I wanted to tell you before, but I was afraid of what Sam might do to me if he found out I told."

"It's OK. I already know," I told her. "And it's not like you think. Trust me."

Coach Duffy's whistle shrilled. "I'll tell you about it later when we go get your dog," I said and ran out onto the court. The moment I'd been dreading was here. My heart started pounding so hard it's a wonder my rib bones didn't rattle.

"OK, here's what we've got!" Coach shouted,

looking at his clipboard. "A-team first. Sam Sherman, you're center. The other starters are Luis Ramez, Tony Anzaldi, Zack Zeno and …"

I took a deep breath and held it.

"LaMar Watson. Congratulations, guys!"

My breath came out in a gasp. I felt dizzy, like I might keel over. I hadn't made it! I hadn't made starter. I probably hadn't made the A-team at all. A burning heat that started somewhere around the soles of my feet, spread across my chest and crept up my neck.

"Way to go, Mickey!" Luis Ramez yelled, slapping me on the back and holding up his hand to high-five me.

I just stared at him.

"You're sixth man, buddy! Didn't you hear?" he asked.

"Yeah, sure," I said, giving him the overdue high-five. I had been so numb with shock, I'd never heard a word after Coach announced the starters.

Sixth man. That meant I'd be the first guy to play when one of the starters came out of the game. I would be an official A-team member. I'd play in almost every game. But it wasn't the same as being a starter. It was like being the magician's assistant instead of the magician.

I knew I should congratulate Luis, Zack, and

the rest of the guys, but I was too stunned.

"Hey, there, little buddy." A large warm hand squeezed the back of my neck.

I turned around. Mike Sherman grinned down at me. "Nice work!" he said, giving me another squeeze.

"B-b-b-b-b-ut I didn't make starter," I said. My voice cracked. The thought of crying in front of a future NBA pro turned my face redder than a can of Classic Coke.

Mike didn't seem to notice. "It won't be long," he said. "You're one lucky guy, Mickey McGhee. You're the underdog. Everybody loves the underdog, especially when he's a little scrapper like you are. You're gonna be a star, buddy. Wait and see."

He went over to congratulate his brother. A little scrapper. That's what Dr. Barry had called the puppy that had outsmarted her by living. I looked around and saw Zack watching me. Slowly, I walked over to where he was standing.

"You did good," I told him.

"Congratulations."

"You did too," he mumbled, looking over my head somewhere. It felt weird between us, like we hardly knew each other.

"Yeah, I guess," I agreed. I was staring at the second-to-the-top button of his striped shirt. A little piece had broken off, leaving a sharp, jagged looking edge. " I ..."

"Listen, Mick..." Zack started at exactly the same time.

We both stopped and laughed, embarrassed at how strange it was not to feel like best friends. "Me first," I said finally. "I just want you to know that I gave Trish the girl dog. The other big one's yours, if you want it."

Zack's dark eyes lit up. "You mean it?" he asked. "Because I was just going to tell you that I acted like a jerk before. The girl dog's great."

"Sure, she is," I agreed. "And Trish likes her already. But the big guy is for you. You can get him today. I'm going to get my dog today too."

All of a sudden I couldn't wait. I knew exactly what I was going to name him. Forget Shaq and Magic. I was going to call my dog Muggsy after Muggsy Bogues, the shortest player in the NBA. The three of us had a lot in common. "Want to come with me to get him now?" I asked.

"You bet I do!" Zack said, bounding toward the door.

I grabbed my jacket, hollered congratulations to Luis and Tony, and followed my best friend out of the gym. We hopped on our bikes and rode past Sam Sherman who was climbing into the front seat of his brother's flashy, red car.

"See ya at practice, Sam!" I hollered.

Sam didn't answer, but Zack looked back over his shoulder at me.

"Hey, watch where you're going!" I yelled at him. "You almost met that telephone pole up close and personal."

We crossed the street and sped toward Arvin Avenue. I looked up at the bright sun and started whistling "Yankee Doodle."

Maybe things hadn't worked out exactly the way I'd wanted them to, but I had a feeling my mom was right. About praying and letting God decide what's best, I mean. Now that Wooster Street Rule—that's a *whole* other story!